Jack
and the
Dragon's Tooth

by
Lily Hyde

Illustrated by Tom Percival

First published in 2007 in Great Britain by
Barrington Stoke Ltd
18 Walker St, Edinburgh, EH3 7LP

www.barringtonstoke.co.uk

ISBN: 978-1-84299-513-6

Printed in Great Britain by Bell & Bain Ltd

Contents

Chapter 1
Two Brothers

There was a king, and he was getting old. Soon, he knew, he would have to hand over his kingdom to one of his sons. But which one? His two sons were always fighting like all brothers fight, only ten times worse. He was afraid that when he died they would fight over his kingdom.

The king began to worry so much that he couldn't eat and he couldn't sleep. At last he woke up his son Peter one morning, and they went for a walk together by the sea.

They walked a long way, picking up shells and paddling in the waves, until they had left the roads and houses far behind.

They sat down on the sand for a drink and a bacon sandwich, and the king said to Peter, "Son, I want to ask you a question. When you are king after I die, how will you treat your brother?"

"My brother is so clever," Peter said, "that I'll ask him to help me rule the kingdom as my minister."

The king thought that was a very good answer. He and Peter finished eating their sandwiches and walked back home together.

The next day the king woke up his second son Jack in the morning, and took him for a walk by the sea. They walked along, throwing stones into the water, until they had left the houses and the roads far behind.

They sat down for a drink and a sandwich, and the king said to Jack, "Son, I want to ask you something. When you are king, how will you treat your brother?"

"My brother is such a fool," said Jack, "that I'll send him to the pig-sty, and I'll teach his wife a lesson she'll never forget."

The king didn't like that answer at all! He waited until Jack walked down to the waves to throw his bread crusts to the sea-gulls. Then he crept up behind him and pushed him into the sea. *Better my son Jack drowns than lives to do such wicked things!* he said to himself.

****

The water was deep and the waves were high. They pulled Jack this way and pushed

3

him that way, and then they dragged him down to the bottom of the sea. At the sea bottom a huge whale was swimming along. It opened its mouth which was as big as a house, and gulped Jack down without even knowing it.

The whale's belly was as big as inside a castle, and it was full of riches and rubbish from the bottom of the sea. When the whale gulped down a ship full of oranges and nuts, Jack lived on oranges and peanuts for a month. When the whale gulped down a cart full of ham, Jack ate ham for three months. At last the whale gulped a fishing boat down. Inside it Jack found a pipe, a flint and a bag of tobacco. He filled the pipe with tobacco and lit it with a spark from the flint. He smoked three pipes one after the other. The whale felt so dizzy and dozy from the smoke that it swam to a beach and fell asleep.

Jack began to crawl out of the whale's belly and up into its gullet. He pushed and he squeezed, he squeezed and he heaved. At last he squeezed right out of the whale's mouth and onto the beach. He was all alone, and he had nothing on at all, because while he'd been inside the whale all his clothes had rotted away.

Jack felt very sorry for himself. He sat down and asked himself, *What shall I do?* Then he started to think about his home and his brother Peter. *I wonder where Peter is now*, he thought, *and if he misses me at all?*

Just then a young king on a horse came along the beach, with ten soldiers behind him. The king stopped when he saw a man without any clothes on, sitting as bare as a new-born baby on the sand. He said to one of his soldiers, "Bring that man to me."

The soldier brought Jack in front of the king. The king didn't think he had ever seen the man with no clothes, but Jack knew the king at once, because it was his brother Peter.

"Good morning," the king said. "Who are you?"

"You can call me No-clothes Jack. And who are you?"

"I'm King Peter. My father is dead, my brother is drowned, and now I'm out looking for a wife."

"I won't wish you luck," said No-clothes Jack. "Because without me to help you, there'll be no wedding for you."

Peter's soldiers thought that was no way to talk to a king. But King Peter couldn't help but like and trust No-clothes Jack. "You'd better come along with me then," Peter said.

He gave No-clothes Jack a pair of trousers to wear, and a horse to ride.

"You must listen to me and do what I say," No-clothes Jack told him. "Then we'll find you a wife and get back to your kingdom safe and sound. But if you don't do what I say, things will turn out badly for both of us."

So King Peter promised he would always listen and do what No-clothes Jack told him.

Chapter 2
Three Armies

Peter and his soldiers came to a valley. It was full of an army of mice. There were so many mice that it looked as if the ground itself had come alive and was hurrying and scurrying along. King Peter didn't much like mice. He rode on with his soldiers, ready to crush the mice under the horses' hooves.

"Stop!" said No-clothes Jack. "You mustn't touch the mice. You must throw them all the cheese in your bags."

"What for?" asked King Peter in surprise.

"Didn't you promise to always do what I say?"

"Oh yes, I did," Peter said. Peter thought No-clothes Jack's words were silly, but he and his soldiers let the mice pass. They threw them all the cheese they had packed away in their bags.

The army of mice ate up the cheese quicker than you could smile, and ran on down the road. The last mouse said to No-clothes Jack, "Many thanks! You've helped me and my brothers. Perhaps one day I'll help you and yours."

Peter and his soldiers were in a bad mood that evening, because there was just bread for supper, without any cheese.

The next day they came to a river. It was full of an army of fish. There were so many fish that you could pick them out of the water just like picking cherries from a tree. King Peter and his soldiers started thinking nice hungry thoughts of fried fish for supper. They jumped off their horses, ready to catch as many as they could.

"Stop!" said No-clothes Jack. "You mustn't touch the fish. You must throw them all the bread in your bags."

"What for?" asked King Peter crossly.

"Didn't you promise to always do what I tell you?"

Peter thought No-clothes Jack was being very odd. But he and his soldiers left the fish alone. They threw them all the bread they had left in their bags.

The army of fish ate up the bread quicker than you could wink, and swam on down the river. The last fish said to No-clothes Jack,

"Thanks for helping me and my brothers. If you need me, one day I'll help you and yours."

That evening King Peter and his soldiers were very grumpy, because there wasn't even any bread for supper.

The third day they rode into a wood. Under the trees was an army of mosquitoes. There were so many mosquitoes, it seemed as if the air itself in the wood was whining and buzzing and black. Peter and his soldiers flapped their arms to wave them away and squash as many as they could.

"Stop!" said No-clothes Jack. "You mustn't harm the mosquitoes. You must let them bite you."

"What?" asked King Peter, amazed. He wondered if No-clothes Jack was mad. But he had promised, and so he and his soldiers stopped squashing the mosquitoes. They hid

their faces in their hats, and put their hands in their pockets so they wouldn't get bitten. But No-clothes Jack had no shirt on, and he sat on his hands so he would not squash a single mosquito even by mistake. Quicker than you could scream, the mosquitoes had bitten him all over.

The army flew on, and the last mosquito said to No-clothes Jack, "Thank you! You've helped me and my brothers. If you call, I'll come and help you and yours."

That night Peter and his soldiers were very cross indeed. They were starving, and No-clothes Jack kept them awake all night scratching his mosquito bites.

****

On they rode, until they came to a castle. All round it was a metal fence with a gate. The gate was made of human bones. The fence was made of iron posts. Each post had a human skull on top of it, except for twelve posts just next to the gate.

"Do you think those twelve posts are waiting for our heads to be put on top of them?" King Peter said, with a shiver.

"We'll see about that," said No-clothes Jack.

The owner of the castle came out to meet them. He was a green-skinned dragon with yellow eyes. "Come in!" he said. "You're just in time for supper."

The dragon's castle was as big as the whale's belly, and full of gold and junk from the dragon's travels round the world. The dragon sat down to dinner with King Peter and his soldiers at a long table. The dragon's twelve daughters sat on the other side of the table. They didn't look like the dragon at all. They were pink-cheeked girls with golden hair, each one more beautiful than the one before. King Peter couldn't stop looking at them.

The dragon said to Peter, "Which of my daughters do you think is the most beautiful?"

"The youngest," said King Peter. "And I'd like to marry her."

"Oh, it's like that, is it?" said the dragon. "Well, I don't mind. I have three tasks that need doing. If you complete all three tasks, you can marry my daughter. But if you fail, there are twelve empty posts in my fence, and I'll put your head and the heads of your soldiers on top of them."

Peter agreed at once.

Chapter 3
The Dragon's Tasks

The next evening the dragon told Peter the first task.

"All my corn, oats and barley are in my barn. I just need you to sort them out into three piles by morning. There must not be one oat in with the corn, not one grain of corn in the barley, nor a bit of barley in with the oats. If I find just one grain out of place, your head and the heads of your soldiers will be on top of my fence posts."

Peter went to look in the barn. The oats, corn and barley were all mixed up in a pile so huge that he couldn't see the top. Peter sat down and began sorting out the three different grains.

An hour passed. He had sorted out a pile of oats as big as your fist, a heap of corn you could eat in one spoonful, and a bunch of barley you could hide under your shoe.

This task is impossible! Peter said to himself. He went outside and started to cry.

"You don't look very happy," said No-clothes Jack, when he saw King Peter.

"How can I help it?" Peter said. "I'll never marry the dragon's daughter, and we will lose our heads tomorrow!" And he told No-clothes Jack what the dragon had asked him to do.

"I should go to bed and sleep on it," No-clothes Jack said. "Morning is always wiser than evening."

King Peter went to bed. He was so tired from sorting the grain in the barn that he soon fell asleep.

No-clothes Jack stood in the yard by the barn and whistled. Before long a mouse came running up to him.

"What is it, No-clothes Jack?" squeaked the mouse.

"I need your help," No-clothes Jack replied. "All the oats, corn and barley in this barn must be sorted into three piles, with not one grain out of place. If it's not done by morning, I and my brother and his soldiers will die."

"That's easy!" said the mouse. The rest of the mouse army came running, and they spent all night sorting the dragon's grain.

****

When King Peter woke up, he didn't feel any wiser in the morning than he had the evening before. But he went to the barn. He couldn't believe it! There were three big neat piles of oats, corn and barley, and No-clothes Jack sitting next to them.

The dragon couldn't believe it either. He sent his twelve daughters to look through the piles for a grain that was out of place. But though they looked very hard, they did not find even one oat in with the corn, nor a grain of corn in with the barley, nor a bit of barley in with the oats.

"Very good," said the dragon, annoyed.

That evening he told Peter the second task.

"My youngest daughter was swimming when she lost her red ruby ring in the river. I need you to find the ring for me, because she loves it more than anything. Bring it to me by morning. If you don't, I'll put your head and the heads of your soldiers on my fence posts."

Peter went down to the river. It was wide and deep and fast-flowing. He took off his shoes and splashed out into the water with a net, to look for the ring.

An hour passed. He had found a pile of stones, a heap of snail-shells, a broken cup and an old boot.

This task is impossible! Peter said to himself. He splashed back to the river bank and started to cry.

"You look upset," said No-clothes Jack, walking past.

"How can I help it?" Peter sniffed. "I'll never marry the dragon's daughter now, and we will lose our heads!" And he told No-clothes Jack what the dragon had asked him to do.

"Why don't you go to bed and sleep on it," No-clothes Jack said. "Morning is always wiser than evening."

King Peter went to bed. He was so tired from looking for the ring in the water that he soon fell asleep.

No-clothes Jack stood on the river bank and whistled. Before long a fish came swimming up to him.

"What is it, No-clothes Jack?" asked the fish.

"I need your help," No-clothes Jack replied. "The dragon's daughter has lost her red ruby ring in the water. If I don't have it by morning, I and my brother and his soldiers will die."

"That's easy!" said the fish. The fish army spent all night hunting through the weeds and mud in the river, looking for the ruby ring.

****

When King Peter woke up in the morning, he didn't feel much wiser than he had the evening before. But he went to the river. He couldn't believe it! No-clothes Jack was sitting there with the ruby ring.

The dragon couldn't believe it either, when Peter brought him the ring. He held out his hand for it. But Peter said, "No! I'll only give it back to its owner, your youngest daughter."

"All right," said the dragon. "That is your third task. We will have dinner with my twelve daughters this evening. If you can tell which one of them is the youngest and give her the ring, then you can marry her. But if you fail, I'll have all your heads for my fence posts."

King Peter went out into the garden humming a happy little tune.

"You look pleased," said No-clothes Jack.

"I can't help it," Peter said. "I'm going to marry the dragon's daughter!" And he told No-clothes Jack what the dragon had asked him to do. "How can I fail to know which one is the youngest daughter," he said, "when I love her?"

"I'm not so sure about that," said No-clothes Jack. He stood in the garden, and whistled. Before long a mosquito came flying up to him.

"What is it, No-clothes Jack?" the mosquito whined.

"I need your help," No-clothes Jack replied. He told the mosquito about the dragon's last task. "If Peter fails, I will die along with him and all his soldiers."

"That's easy!" said the mosquito. "Here's what we will do …"

Chapter 4

The Dragon's Daughter and No-clothes Jack

That evening, the dragon sat down to dinner with his twelve daughters along one side of the table. Peter stared at them in a panic. The twelve daughters were all wearing the same dresses, with the same blue ribbons in their hair. They all looked the same, from the tops of their golden heads to the tips of their pretty pink toes. Though he stared and stared, Peter simply could not say which one was the youngest daughter.

King Peter walked all the way down past the table. There was nothing at all to tell one daughter from another; even their smiles were the same. *Is it this girl?* he asked himself. *Or is it that girl?*

Peter walked all the way back up along the table. He heard a whining noise.
A mosquito was flying above the heads of the twelve daughters. *Is it the girl in the middle?* Peter thought. *Or is it the girl on the end?*

Peter walked a third time down past the table. The whining noise stopped. The mosquito had landed on the nose of one of the daughters. She quickly flicked it away.

"That's my girl!" Peter cried. He ran to the daughter who had flicked the mosquito from her nose. "Here is your ring," he said. "I looked for it in the river all night!"

The youngest daughter's cheeks blushed even pinker. She put the ruby ring on her finger, and it was a perfect fit.

They were married that same evening. In the middle of the wedding party, No-clothes Jack said to Peter, "We must go right now."

"I don't want to," said Peter. He was enjoying himself.

"Didn't you promise to always do what I say?"

"Oh, all right then." Peter was annoyed. He called together his soldiers, who were dancing with the dragon's daughters. He took his bride's hand, and they ran out of the castle and through the gate.

Behind them came twelve dragons with twelve axes, to chop off the heads of Peter and No-clothes Jack and the soldiers. No-clothes Jack pulled up the twelve empty

fence posts beside the gate, and threw them behind him. The fence posts hit the dragons, and the dragons fell down dead.

****

That's how Peter came back safe and sound to his kingdom with his bride. He was so pleased with No-clothes Jack that he asked him to become his minister and help him rule.

"All right," said No-clothes Jack. "But listen to me. You must never tell your wife what we really did at the dragon's castle. If you do, it'll turn out badly for both of us."

Peter didn't much like these words. He thought perhaps No-clothes Jack felt jealous of his lovely wife.

King Peter was very pleased indeed with the dragon's daughter. He spent all his time with her, and let No-clothes Jack rule the kingdom. The dragon's daughter cooked Peter chocolate cakes. She made him silk shirts. She told him stories about brave, clever heroes. "But none of them are as brave and clever as you, dear husband," she said. "Won't you tell me how you completed the dragon's tasks? That must be the most wonderful story of all."

Peter recalled his promise to always do what No-clothes Jack told him. He said to his wife, "Oh no, I'm much too modest."

The dragon's daughter looked very pretty as she asked him. She was very tender when she asked, and very nice. But Peter would not tell her how he had completed the dragon's tasks.

One day she started to cry. She said, "Dear husband, I've lost my very best needle. Won't you find it for me?"

"Why should I know where it is?" asked Peter in surprise.

"You found my ruby ring when I lost it in the river." The dragon's daughter fluttered her eye-lashes at him. "I thought that finding my needle would be easy for you."

"You'd better ask No-clothes Jack," said King Peter. "For it was him, not me, who found your ring. No-clothes Jack completed all of the dragon's tasks. If it weren't for him, my head would have been on a fence post long ago!"

At once, the dragon's daughter smiled and said, "I'll just pop round and ask him then." She ran to No-clothes Jack's house. But she didn't ask him to find her needle. Instead, she hid a sharp, sharp dragon's tooth in the pocket of his jacket.

No-clothes Jack put on his jacket and went hunting. By the time he came to the hill, the dragon's tooth had worked its way through his pocket. By the time he came to the wood, the dragon's tooth had worked its way through his shirt. No-clothes Jack walked into the wood, when he felt a sharp, sharp pain. It was the dragon's tooth working its way through his skin.

"Peter, you have forgotten your promise to always do what I told you," No-clothes Jack cried out. "Now it will turn out badly for both of us!"

By the time he finished speaking, the dragon's tooth had worked its way into his heart, and it killed him.

Chapter 5
The Dead and Living Water

No-clothes Jack lay dead in the wood. The wild animals would have eaten him up, were it not for the mice and the mosquitoes. The mice ran round so fast, and the mosquitoes buzzed so angrily, that they scared all the animals away. And all the time the dragon's tooth was working and working, because once it had started it could not stop. It worked its way out of No-clothes Jack's heart. It worked all the way down to No-clothes Jack's foot.

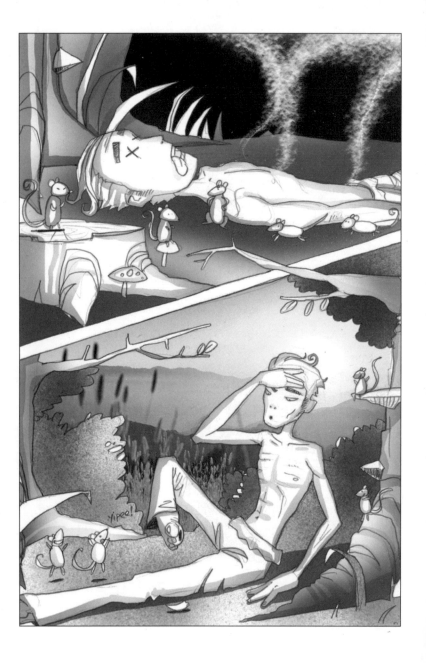

And then it worked its way out of his heel and fell onto the grass.

No-clothes Jack came back to life. But he was only half the man he had been, with a limp in one leg where the dragon's tooth had worked out of his heel. No-clothes Jack put the tooth inside a silver box where he kept his gun-powder. He put the silver box inside an iron box where he kept his bullets. He put the iron box inside a tin box where he kept his tobacco. Then he put the tin box in his pocket.

On the far side of the wood was another kingdom. No-clothes Jack limped into the city and stood outside the church to beg.

On Sunday the princess of that kingdom went to church with her servant girl and a soldier. When the soldier saw No-clothes Jack, he told him to move out of the way. But the princess felt sorry for the young beggar with the limp. She gave him a gold coin out of her pocket.

"Thank you, princess!" said No-clothes Jack. "You've helped me. Now if you'll let me, I'll help you."

The princess was thin and pale. "No one can help me," she replied, with a sigh.

The servant girl ran to the castle and told the king what the beggar had said. The king sent for No-clothes Jack at once.

"My daughter is sick and no one can make her well," the king said. "But you say you can help her. It's hard to believe; you can't even help yourself."

"She isn't sick, she's under a spell," said No-clothes Jack. "Let me stay in her bedroom for one night, and the princess will be better by morning."

"Oh, it's like that, is it?" said the king. "Well, all right then. But if she isn't well by morning I'll put you in prison and let you rot there."

After supper the princess went to bed. Her servant girl sat by the window. Her soldier stood by the door. No-clothes Jack lay down at the foot of the bed, with the tin box from his pocket under his head.

An hour passed, and the princess fell asleep. Another hour passed, and the servant girl nodded her head and fell asleep. A third hour passed, and the soldier leaned against the door, fast asleep.

No-clothes Jack's eye-lids felt so heavy that he propped them open with his fingers. But under his head he could hear the dragon's tooth, working and working its way through the silver box and the iron box and the tin box. That kept him awake all right.

At midnight, a black snake crawled under the bedroom door. When he saw it, No-clothes Jack opened his tin box. He took out the iron box inside.

The snake stood up in the bedroom and turned into a wizard in a black cloak. No-clothes Jack opened the iron box. He took out the silver box inside.

The wizard began to cast a spell on the sleeping princess. No-clothes Jack quickly opened the silver box. He tipped the dragon's tooth inside into the wizard's pocket.

Then he waited until the dragon's tooth worked its way through the wizard's cloak, through his shirt and into his heart and killed him.

The princess woke up the next morning as fresh and bright as the day outside. She kissed No-clothes Jack where he lay at the

foot of her bed. "We'll have to get married now, my dear," she said.

"All right, I don't mind," said No-clothes Jack. "Just let me go and get my wedding clothes."

He took the dead wizard outside, and sat beside him until the dragon's tooth worked its way out of the wizard's thumb. The wizard came back to life. But he was half the man he had been, and he could not use his arm at all.

"Take me to the pools of dead and living water," No-clothes Jack said to the wizard. "Then we can both heal ourselves. And I'll let you go free if you promise never to come near the princess again."

The wizard agreed, even though he didn't much want to. They got two horses and rode to the middle of a great forest. There the pools of dead and living water lay side by side like two mirrors.

"This is the living water," said the wizard, pointing to the pool on the left. "Please, after you."

"Oh no, after you," said No-clothes Jack.

"No, no, I insist, you first," said the wizard.

"No, you first!" said No-clothes Jack, pushing the wizard into the pool on the left. The wizard curled up and died at once, because the pool was full of dead water.

"I thought so," said No-clothes Jack. He washed in the pool on the right, which was full of living water. The living water didn't just heal his limp. It turned him into the strongest, most handsome man you ever saw. No-clothes Jack rode back to the city, and next Sunday in the church he and the princess were married.

Chapter 6
The King and the Swine-herd

No-clothes Jack became king. One day he started to wonder what had happened to his brother Peter. Once he had started thinking, he couldn't sit still until he had found out. He crossed the wood to his brother's kingdom.

The first thing he saw when he got there was a herd of pigs. The pigs were chomping acorns, while the swine-herd who looked after them was sleeping under an oak tree.

"Good morning!" said No-clothes Jack.

The swine-herd woke up. No-clothes Jack couldn't believe it! It was his brother Peter.

"Is that really you, No-clothes Jack?" said Peter. "You look like a king."

"That's because I am a king. Is it really you, Peter, keeping pigs?"

Peter looked at the ground in shame.

"Well, you deserve it," said No-clothes Jack. "Didn't I say you should never tell your wife about the dragon's three tasks?"

"I'm sorry, No-clothes Jack," said Peter. "The dragon's daughter has punished me every day since. She sends me out each morning with the pigs. When I bring them home, I have to kiss the biggest pig on its nose; only then will it go through the gate.

And my wife sits on the door-step drinking tea and making fun of me."

"Never mind," No-clothes Jack said. "If you promise to do as I say, today is the last day she'll make fun of you."

He told Peter to go home and hide in the pig-sty. Then No-clothes Jack put on Peter's hat, and took the pigs home to the castle.

When they came to the castle the biggest pig stood stock-still in the gate-way. No matter how No-clothes Jack pushed and prodded, it would not go through the gate.

The dragon's daughter was sitting on the door-step, slurping her tea.

"Here comes my fool of a husband," she said. "Hurry up and kiss the pig, dear husband, so it will go through the gate."

"Are you sure you want me to?" said No-clothes Jack.

"Of course I'm sure!" said the dragon's daughter. She laughed so much she spilt her tea.

"All right." No-clothes Jack kissed the pig on its nose. At once it grunted and went through the gate. Behind it came a huge army of mice. They swarmed onto the door-step and began to bite the dragon's daughter as hard as they could on her ankles and toes.

"Help!" shouted the dragon's daughter. She dropped the cup and ran into the castle, slamming the door. Through the castle windows came an army of mosquitoes. They flew at the dragon's daughter and began to bite her as hard as they could on her ears and nose.

"Help!" bawled the dragon's daughter. She ran out of the castle and jumped into the river to try and escape. The river was full of an army of fish. They swam round the dragon's daughter and began to bite her as hard as they could on her knees and elbows.

"Help!" yelled the dragon's daughter, splashing and flapping about in the water.

In the pig-sty, King Peter heard all the noise. He jumped up and ran to see what was happening. When he saw his wife in the river, he pulled her out at once.

The dragon's daughter was half-drowned and bitten all over. "Thank you, dear husband," she said to Peter. "I promise I'll never make fun of you again."

Peter was very pleased to have No-clothes Jack back. "You're so clever," he said, "won't you be my minister again and help me rule the kingdom?"

"No, I won't, because I'm a king myself now," said No-clothes Jack. "Didn't I say that when I was king I would send you to the pig-sty, and teach your wife a lesson she'd never forget?"

"What?" said Peter, amazed.

"I said you were a fool as well," No-clothes Jack said. "And you still are, brother, as it's taken you so long to work out who I am!"

Then at long last King Peter saw that it was his brother Jack, who he'd thought was drowned in the sea.

That's how Jack's words to his father by the sea came true after all. No-clothes Jack went back to the princess on the other side of the wood, but sometimes he helped rule Peter's kingdom as well as his own. The dragon's daughter became a very good wife after that. She sometimes still made fun of King Peter though, because he never did get much wiser. The two brothers lived happily with their wives, and they never fought with each other again as long as they lived.

BATTLE CARDS

Lily Hyde

Author

Favourite hero:
Sir Gawain, one of King Arthur's Knights.

Favourite monster:
Dragons (and their daughters).

Your weapon of choice:
Seven-league boots (so I could run away very quickly).

Special secret power:
Vanishing in a second.

Goodie or baddie:
The baddie who turns out at the end to be the goodie.

WHO WILL WIN?

Tom Percival

Illustrator

Favourite hero:
He-Man

Favourite monster:
Skeletor (from He-Man)

Your weapon of choice:
Hopefully something more useful than my wits!

Favourite fight scene:
Me and Ben Colfield aged 4 on our first day at Primary School.

Goodie or baddie:
Well, I should say the goodie, but they're nearly always a bit dull aren't they?

RELOADED

Barrington Stoke would like to thank all its readers for commenting on the manuscript before publication and in particular:

Rowan Chalmers

Micheál Murphy

Keith Rogerson

Become a Consultant!

Would you like to give us feedback on our titles before they are published? Contact us at the email address below – we'd love to hear from you!

info@barringtonstoke.co.uk
www.barringtonstoke.co.uk